# THE LITTLE
# BOOK OF
# VALUES

Copyright © 1996 by
Random House Value Publishing, Inc.
All rights reserved.

This 1996 edition is published by
Glorya Hale Books,
an imprint of Random House Value
Publishing, Inc.,
40 Engelhard Avenue, Avenel, New
Jersey 07001.

*Edited by Carol Kelly Gangi*
*Production supervised by Ellen Reed*
*Designed by Liz Trovato*

Random House
New York • Toronto • London •
Sydney • Auckland

Printed and bound in Malaysia

A CIP catalog record for this book is
available from the Library of Congress.

ISBN 0–517–14979–6

8 7 6 5 4 3 2 1

# THE LITTLE
# BOOK OF
# VALUES

MORAL FABLES
BY LAURA E. RICHARDS

RHYMES FOR KINDLY CHILDREN
BY FAIRMONT SNYDER

ILLUSTRATED
BY JOHN B. GRUELLE

GHB
GLORYA HALE BOOKS
NEW YORK • AVENEL

# CONTENTS

Introduction 7

Preface 9

The Golden Windows 10

Good and Bad Visitors 17

Two Ways 18

Timothy Timkins 20

The Wheat Field 22

The Kindly Rule 27

The Coming of the King 28

The Courteous Favorite 33

The Great Feast 34

Slow-Poke and Dilly-Dally 39

The Pig Brother 40

The Careless Nail Biter 45

The Hill 46

The Tired Girl 48

About Angels 50

The Little Fibber  56

The Apron String  58

Never-Tells and Tattle-Tales  62

The Sailor Man  64

Shameless Abel  69

The Road  70

The Little Stay-Up  74

The Willing Practicer  75

Child's Play  76

Susan Kindly's Party  79

A Misunderstanding  80

The Orderly Twins  83

The Stars  84

The Sleep Angel  87

# INTRODUCTION

*The Little Book of Values* will take you and your family back to the early years of the twentieth century, to a time when every children's story taught a lesson and every poem was instructive.

The stories, or fables, in this little book were written by Laura E. Richards. When they were first published they were read and reread by young and old. "The House with the Golden Windows," is considered a classic and appeared in schoolbooks for at least fifty years after it was written. In Ms. Richards' stories you'll meet kind and helpful angels, plants and animals that can speak, and many bad as well as good children.

Fairmont Snyder's poems were originally collected in the popular book *Rhymes for Kindly Children*. A selection of these charming verses is included here. They will introduce you to many young people—very smart Timothy Timkins, Virginia, who was always courteous, Alice, who bit her nails, Susan Kindly, who gave an unusual party, and the orderly twins, Ray and May.

The delightful illustrations were done by John B. Gruelle the creator of Raggedy Ann and Andy.

This lovely collection of moral fables and instructive poems is designed to make today's boys and girls, and their mothers and fathers, aware of the family values that were instilled in everyone when the world was a better place in which to live.

# PREFACE

So many things a child should know!
But first he ought to learn
That Kindly Children live to LOVE
And JOY is their return.

Now he who would be very kind,
Perceives his brother's needs,
And every signal of distress
His living spirit heeds.

Those children who are taught to LOVE
And call all creatures "Brothers,"
Soon grow to be more thoughtful
Of their mothers and all others.

# The Golden Windows

ll day long the little boy worked hard, in field and barn and shed, for his parents were poor farmers and could not pay a workman. But at sunset there came an hour that was all his own, for his father had given it to him. Then the boy would go up to the top of a hill and look across at another hill that rose some miles away. On this far hill stood a house with windows of clear gold and diamonds. They shone and blazed so that it made the boy wink to look at them, but after awhile the people in the house put up shutters, as it seemed, and then it looked like any common farmhouse. The boy supposed they did this because it was

supper time. Then he would go into the house and have his supper of bread and milk, and so to bed.

One day the boy's father called him and said, "You have been a good boy, and have earned a holiday. Take this day for your own, but remember that God gave it, and try to learn some good thing."

The boy thanked his father and kissed his mother. Then he put a piece of bread in his pocket, and started off to find the house with the golden windows.

It was pleasant walking. His bare feet made marks in the white dust, and when he looked back, the footprints seemed to be following him, and making company for him. His shadow, too, kept beside him, and would dance or run with him as he pleased; so it was very cheerful.

By and by he felt hungry. He sat down next to a brook that ran through the alder hedge by the roadside, and ate his bread, and drank the clear water. Then he scattered the crumbs for the birds, as his mother had taught him to do, and went on his way.

After a long time he came to a high green hill. When he had climbed the hill, there was the house on the top; but it seemed that the shutters were up, for he could not see the golden windows. He came up to the house, and then he could well have wept, for the windows were of clear glass, like any others, and there was no gold anywhere about them.

A woman came to the door, and looked kindly at the boy, and asked him what he wanted.

"I saw the golden windows from our

hilltop," he said, "and I came to see them, but now they are only glass."

The woman shook her head and laughed.

"We are poor farming people," she said, "and are not likely to have gold about our windows, but glass is better to see through."

She bade the boy sit down on the broad stone step at the door, and brought him a cup of milk and a cake, and bade him rest. Then she called her daughter, a child of his own age, and nodded kindly at the two, and went back to her work.

The little girl was barefooted like himself, and wore a brown cotton dress, but her hair was golden like the windows he had seen, and her eyes were blue like the sky at noon. She led the boy about the farm, and showed him her black calf with the white star on its forehead. He told her about his own calf at home, which was red like a chestnut, with four white feet. Then when they had eaten an apple together, and so had become friends, the boy asked her about the golden windows. The little girl nodded and said she knew all about them, only he had mistaken the house.

"You have come quite the wrong way!" she said. "Come with me, and I will show you the house with the golden windows, and then you will see for yourself."

They went to a knoll that rose behind the farmhouse, and as they went the little girl told him that the golden windows could only be seen at a certain hour, about sunset.

"Yes, I know that!" said the boy.

When they reached the top of the knoll, the girl turned and pointed. There on a hill far away stood a house with windows of clear gold and diamond, just as he had seen them. And when they looked again, the boy saw that it was his own home.

Then he told the little girl that he must go. He gave her his best pebble, the white one with the red band, that he had carried for a year in his pocket. She gave him three horse chestnuts, one red like satin, one spotted, and one white like milk. He kissed her, and promised to come again, but he did not tell her what he had learned; and so he went back down the hill, and the little girl stood in the sunset light and watched him.

The way home was long, and it was dark before the boy reached his father's house, but the lamplight and firelight shone through the windows, making them almost as bright as he had seen them from the hilltop. When he opened the door, his mother came to kiss him, and his little sister ran to throw her arms about his neck, and his father looked up and smiled from his seat by the fire.

"Have you had a good day?" asked his mother.

"Yes", said the boy. "I have had a very good day."

"And have you learned anything?" asked his father.

"Yes!" said the boy. "I have learned that our house has windows of gold and diamond."

# Good and Bad Visitors

Some little boys such rowdies are,
While some are perfect gentlemen:
Of one they say: "I'm glad he's gone"—
The other they ask back again.

When Henry's mother takes him out
To tea or make a call, you know,
He fidgets all the time and cries:
"Oh, let's go home, I want to go!"

But Dick is such a different lad,
he does not touch the bric-a-brac,
He never cries or interrupts,
And so they always ask him back.

# Two Ways

wo little weeds grew on a bank by the roadside. All summer they had drunk dew and sunshine, and had been happy, but now the autumn had come, with gray skies and winds that nipped and pinched them.

"We shall die soon!" said one little weed. "I should like to do something pleasant before I die, just to show what a happy time I have had. I think I will turn red, and then people will see how I feel."

"You will be a great fool to waste your strength in any such nonsense!" said the other little weed. "I shall live as long as I can, and hug the brown bank here."

So the first little weed turned bright

scarlet, and was so pretty that everyone who passed that way turned to look at it. By and by there came along a most beautiful maiden with her lover. When the lover saw the scarlet leaves, he plucked them, and set them in his maiden's hair, and they lent her a new grace. This made the little weed so happy that he died for pure joy.

The second little weed lived on and turned slowly brown, like the bank.

"He was a fool!" he said, speaking of his companion. "He put all his strength into turning red, and so he died."

"I was proud of him!" said the brown bank. "He did what he could and people observed him."

"Yes, but I am alive and stay with you!" said the weed.

"Much I care!" said the brown bank.

# TIMOTHY TIMKINS

Timothy Timkins is very smart,
He thinks with his head, and he thinks
    with his heart;
He is very polite to his sister and brother,
And jumps up to give his own chair to
    his mother.

# THE WHEAT FIELD

ome children were set to reap in a wheat field. The wheat was yellow as gold, the sun shone gloriously, and the butterflies flew hither and thither. Some of the children worked better, and some worse; but there was one who ran here and there after the butterflies that fluttered about his head. He sang as he ran.

By and by evening came, and the Angel of the wheat field called to the children and said, "Come now to the gate, and bring your sheaves of wheat with you."

So the children came, bringing their sheaves. Some had great piles, laid close and even, so that they might carry more.

Some had theirs laid large and loose, so that they looked more than they were. But one, the child that had run to and fro after the butterflies, came empty-handed.

The Angel said to this child, "Where are your sheaves?"

The child hung his head. "I do not know!" he said. "I had some, but I have lost them, I know not how."

"No one may enter without sheaves," said the Angel.

"I know that," said the child. "But I thought I would like to see the place where the others were going. Besides, they would not let me leave them."

Then all the other children cried out together. One said, "Dear Angel, let him in! In the morning I was sick and this child came and played with me, and showed me the butterflies, and I forgot my pain. Also, he gave me one of his sheaves, and I would give it to him again, but I cannot tell it now from my own."

Another said, "Dear Angel, let him in! At noon the sun beat on my head so fiercely that I fainted and fell down like one dead; and this child came running by, and when he saw me he brought water to revive me, and then he showed me the butterflies, and was so glad and merry that my strength returned. To me also he gave one of his sheaves, and I would give it to him again, but it is so like my own that I cannot tell it."

And a third child said, "Just now, as evening was coming, I was weary and sad, and had so few sheaves that it seemed hardly worth my while to go on working. But this child comforted me, and showed me the butterflies, and gave me of his sheaves. Look! It may be that this was his; and yet I cannot tell, it is so like my own."

And all the children said, "We also had sheaves of his, dear Angel. Let him in, we pray you!"

The Angel smiled, and reached his hand inside the gate and brought out a pile of sheaves. It was not a large pile, but the glory of the sun was on it so that it seemed to lighten the whole field.

"Here are his sheaves!" said the Angel. "They are known and counted, every one." And he said to the child, "Lead the way in!"

# THE KINDLY RULE

My teacher says that animals
Deserve the best of fare:
Clean beds, fresh water, healthful food
And very loving care.

And when their eyes look up to me,
Such deep and trusting eyes—
I wonder how could one forget
Or treat them otherwise!

# THE COMING OF THE KING

ome children were at play in their playground one day, when a herald rode through the town, blowing a trumpet, and crying aloud, "The King! The King passes by this road today. Make ready for the King!"

The children stopped their play and looked at one another.

"Did you hear that?" they said. "The King is coming. He may look over the wall and see our playground. Who knows? We must put it in order."

The playground was sadly dirty, and in the corners were scraps of paper and broken toys, for these were careless children. But now, one brought a hoe and another a

rake and a third ran to fetch the wheelbar-
row from behind the garden gate. They
labored hard, until at length all was clean
and tidy.

"Now it is clean!" they said, "but we must
make it pretty, too, for kings are used to fine
things. Maybe he would not notice mere
cleanness, for he may have it all the time."

Then one brought sweet rushes and
strewed them on the ground. Others made
garlands of oak leaves and pine tassels and
hung them on the walls. The littlest one
pulled marigold buds and threw them all
about the playground, "to look like gold,"
he said.

When all was done the playground was
so beautiful that the children stood and
looked at it, and clapped their hands with
pleasure.

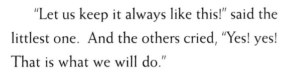

"Let us keep it always like this!" said the littlest one. And the others cried, "Yes! yes! That is what we will do."

They waited all day for the coming of the King, but he never came; only, toward sunset, a man with travel worn clothes, and a kind, tired face passed along the road and stopped to look over the wall.

"What a pleasant place!" said the man. "May I come in and rest, dear children?"

The children brought him in gladly, and set him on the seat that they had made from an old cask. They had covered it with an old red cloak to make it look like a throne, and it made a very good one.

"It is our playground!" they said. "We made it pretty for the King, but he did not come, and now we mean to keep it so for ourselves."

"That is good!" said the man.

"Because we think pretty and clean is nicer than ugly and dirty!" said another.

"That is better!" said the man.

"And for tired people to rest in!" said the littlest one.

"That is best of all!" said the man.

He sat and rested, and looked at the children with such kind eyes that they gathered around him and told him all they knew: about the five puppies in the barn, and the thrush's nest with four blue eggs, and the shore where they found beautiful gold shells. The man nodded and understood all about it.

By and by he asked for a cup of water, and they brought it to him in the best cup, with the gold sprigs on it. After he drank the water he thanked the children, and rose

31

and went on his way. But before he went he laid his hand on their heads for a moment, and the touch went warm to their hearts.

The children stood by the wall and watched the man as he went slowly along. The sun was setting and the light fell in long slanting rays across the road.

"He looks so tired!" said one of the children.

"But he was so kind!" said another.

"See!" said the littlest one. "How the sun shines on his hair! It makes it look like a crown of gold."

# THE COURTEOUS FAVORITE

Little Virginia everyone likes
Her heart is kind and true:
She always says "please" for everything,
And always says "thank you," too.
And just for the very slightest mistake
She quickly begs pardon of you.

# THE GREAT FEAST

ne day the Play Angel came into a nursery where four little children sat on the floor with sad and troubled faces. "What is the matter, dears?" asked the Play Angel.

"We wanted to have a grand feast!" said the child whose nursery it was.

"Yes, that would be delightful!" said the Play Angel.

"But there is only one cookie!" said the child whose nursery it was.

"And it is a very small cookie!" said the child who was a cousin, and therefore felt a right to speak.

"Not big enough for myself!" said the child whose nursery it was.

The other two children said nothing, because they were not relations, but they looked at the cookie with large eyes, and their mouths went up in the middle and down at the sides.

"Well," said the Play Angel, "suppose we have a feast just the same! I think we can manage it."

She broke the cookie into four pieces and gave one piece to the littlest child.

"See!" she said. "This is a roast chicken. It is just as brown and crispy as it can be, and there is cranberry sauce on one side, and on the other a little mountain of mashed potatoes. It must be a volcano, it smokes so. Do you see?"

"Yes!" said the littlest one. His mouth went down in the middle and up at the corners.

The Play Angel gave a piece to the next child. "Here," she said, "is a little pie! Outside, as you see, it is brown and crusty, with a wreath of pastry leaves around the edge and 'For You' in the middle; but inside it is all chicken and ham and jelly and hard-boiled eggs. Did ever you see such a pie?"

"I never did!" said the child.

"Now here," said the Angel to the third child, "is a round cake. *Look* at it! The frosting is half an inch thick, with candied rose leaves and angelica laid on in true-lovers' knots; and inside there are chopped-up almonds, and raisins, and great slices of citron. It is the prettiest cake I ever saw, and the best."

"So it is!" said the third child.

Then the Angel gave the last piece to the child whose nursery it was.

"My dear!" she said. "Just look! Here is an ice-cream rabbit. He is snow-white outside, with eyes of tiny red candies. See his ears, and his little snubby tail! But inside, I *think* you will find him pink. Now, when I clap my hands and count one, two, three, you must eat up all the feast. One–two–three!"

So the children ate up all the feast.

"There!" said the Angel. "Did ever you see such a grand feast?"

"No, we never did!" said all the four children together.

"And there are some crumbs left over," said the Angel. "Come, and we will give them to the brother birds!"

"But you didn't have any!" said the child whose nursery it was.

"Oh, yes!" said the Angel. "I had it all!"

# SLOW-POKE
# AND DILLY-DALLY

Slow-Poke and Dilly-Dally
Why do you lag back so?
You're always half an hour late,
Everywhere you go.
If you would only stop to think,
You'd know that it is wrong;
How would YOU like to sit and wait,
While some old Slow-Poke drags along?

# THE PIG BROTHER

There was once a child who was untidy. He left his books on the floor and his muddy shoes on the table. He put his fingers in the jam and spilled ink on his best shirt. There was really no end to his untidiness.

One day the Tidy Angel came into his nursery. "This will never do!" said the Angel. "This is really shocking. You must go out and stay with your brother while I straighten up here."

"I have no brother!" said the child.

"Yes, you have!" said the Angel. "You may not know him, but he will know you. Go out in the garden and watch for him, and he will soon come."

"I don't know what you mean!" said the child, but he went out into the garden and waited.

Presently a squirrel came along, whisking his tail.

"Are you my brother?" asked the child.

The squirrel looked him over carefully. "Well, I should hope not!" he said. "My fur is neat and smooth, my nest is handsomely made, and in perfect order, and my young ones are properly brought up. Why do you insult me by asking such a question?"

He whisked off and the child waited.

Presently a wren came hopping by.

"Are you my brother?" asked the child.

"No indeed!" said the wren. "What impertinence! You will find no tidier person than I in the whole garden. Not a feather is out of place, and my eggs are the wonder of all for smoothness and beauty. Brother, indeed!" He hopped off, ruffling his feathers, and the child waited.

By and by a large tomcat came along.

"Are you my brother?" asked the child.

"Go and look at yourself in the glass," said the tomcat haughtily, "and you will have your answer. I have been washing myself in the sun all the morning, while it is clear that no water has come near you for a long time. There are no such creatures as you in my family, I am humbly thankful to say."

He walked on, waving his tail, and the child waited.

Presently a pig came trotting along.

The child did not wish to ask the pig if he were his brother, but the pig did not wait to be asked.

"Hello, brother!" he grunted.

"I am not your brother!" said the child.

"Oh, yes, you are!" said the pig. "I confess I am not proud of you, but there is no mistaking the members of our family. Come along, and have a good roll in the barnyard! There is some lovely black mud there."

"I don't like to roll in mud!" said the child.

"Tell that to the hens!" said the pig brother. "Look at your hands, and your shoes, and your shirt! Come along, I say! You may have some of the pig's slop for supper, if there is more than I want."

"I don't want pig's slop!" said the child, and he began to cry.

Just then the Tidy Angel came out.

"I have straightened everything up," she

said, "and so it must stay. Now, will you go with the pig brother, or will you come back with me, and be a tidy child?"

"With you, with you!" cried the child, and he clung to the Angel's dress.

The pig brother grunted. "Small loss!" he said. "There will be all the more slop for me!" and he trotted on.

# The Careless Nail-Biter

Alice bites her fingernails,
Such a dreadful thing to do,
She bites them down until they hurt;
They look so horrid, too.

If she were a careful child,
She'd have her hands look pretty,
But she doesn't seem to care—
Isn't that a pity?

# THE HILL

I cannot walk up this hill," said the little boy. "I cannot possibly do it. What will become of me? I must stay here all my life, at the foot of the hill. It is too terrible!"

"That is a pity!" said his sister. "But look, little boy! I have found such a pleasant thing to play. Take a step, and see how clear a footprint you can make in the dust. Look at mine! Every single line in my foot is printed clear. Now, you try and see if you can do as well!"

The little boy took a step.

"Mine is just as clear! he said.

"Do you think so?" asked his sister. "See mine, again here! I tread harder than you, because I am heavier, and so the print is deeper. Try again."

"*Now* mine is just as deep!" cried the little boy. "See! Here, and here, and here, they are just as deep as they can be."

"Yes, that is very good," said his sister, "but now it is my turn. Let me try again, and we shall see."

They kept on, step by step, matching their footprints and laughing to see the gray dust puff up between their bare toes.

By and by the little boy looked up.

"Why!" he said, "We are at the top of the hill!"

"Dear me!" said the sister. "So we are!"

# THE TIRED GIRL

Jessie May could play all day,
From morning until night;
At tag, I spy, or run-sheep-run,
She raced with all her might.
But when the dishes were not done,
And mother vainly calling,
Sly Jessie May would fade away,
With weariness appalling.

# ABOUT ANGELS

M other," said the child, "are there really angels?"

"The Good Book says so," said the mother.

"Yes," said the child, "I have seen the picture. But did you ever see one, Mother?"

"I think I have," said the mother, "but she was not dressed like the picture."

"I am going to find one!" said the child. "I am going to run along the road, miles, and miles, and miles, until I find an angel."

"That will be a good plan!" said the mother. "And I will go with you, for you are too little to run far alone."

"I am not little anymore!" said the child. "I have trousers. I am big."

"So you are!" said the mother. "I forgot. But it is a fine day and I should like to have a walk."

"But you walk so slowly, with your lame foot."

"I can walk faster than you think!" said the mother.

So they started, the child leaping and running, and the mother stepping out so bravely with her lame foot that the child soon forgot about it.

The child danced on ahead, and presently he saw a chariot coming toward him, drawn by prancing white horses. In the chariot sat a splendid lady in velvet and furs, with white plumes waving above her dark hair. As she moved in her seat, she flashed with jewels and gold, but her eyes were brighter than her diamonds.

"Are you an angel?" asked the child, running up beside the chariot.

The lady made no reply, but stared coldly at the child. Then she spoke a word to her coachman. He flicked his whip, the chariot rolled away swiftly in a cloud of dust, and disappeared.

The dust filled the child's eyes and mouth and made him choke and sneeze. He gasped for breath and rubbed his eyes, but presently his mother came and wiped away the dust with her blue gingham apron.

"That was not an angel!" said the child.

"No, indeed!" said the mother. "Nothing like one!"

The child danced on again, leaping and running from side to side of the road. And the mother followed as best she could.

By and by the child met a most beautiful maiden, clad in a white dress. Her eyes were like blue stars, and the blushes came and went in her face like roses looking through snow.

"I am sure you must be an angel!" cried the child.

The maiden blushed more sweetly than before. "You dear little child!" she cried. Someone else said that, only last evening. Do I really look like an angel?"

"You *are* an angel!" said the child.

The maiden took him up in her arms and kissed him, and held him tenderly.

"You are the dearest little thing I ever saw!" she said. "Tell me what makes you think so!" Then suddenly her face changed.

"Oh!" she cried. "There he is, coming to meet me! And you have soiled my white dress with your dusty shoes and pulled my hair all awry. Run away, child. Go home to your mother!"

She set the child down, not unkindly, but so hastily that he stumbled and fell. She did not see that, for she was hastening forward to meet her lover who was coming along the road. (Now if the maiden had only known, he thought her twice as lovely with the child in her arms. But she did not know.)

The child lay in the dusty road and sobbed until his mother came along and picked him up, and wiped away the tears with her blue gingham apron.

"I don't believe that was an angel after all," he said.

"No!" said the mother. "But she may be one some day. She is young yet."

"I am tired!" said the child. "Will you carry me home, Mother?"

"Why, yes!" said the mother. "That is what I came for."

The child put his arms around his mother's neck, and she held him tight and trudged along the road, singing the song he liked best.

Suddenly he looked up in her face.

"Mother," he said, "I don't suppose *you* could be an angel, could you?"

"Oh, what a foolish child!" said the mother. "Who ever heard of an angel in a blue gingham apron?" And she went on singing, and stepped out so bravely on her lame foot that no one would ever have known she was lame.

# THE LITTLE FIBBER

Mary Ellen told a fib,
Oh, dear me!  Oh, mercy me!
Now she cannot go with us
To Aunt Ruth's to tea.

She will have to stay at home,
And learn to speak the truth;
Think of all the things she'll miss—
At tea with Auntie Ruth!

# THE APRON STRING

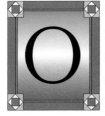

Once upon a time a boy played about the house, running at his mother's side. Since he was very little, his mother tied him to the string of her apron.

"Now," she said, "when you stumble, you can pull yourself up by the apron string, and so you will not fall."

The boy did that, and all went well, and the mother sang at her work.

By and by the boy grew so tall that his head came above the windowsill. Looking through the window, he saw far away green trees waving, and a flowing river that flashed in the sun, and, rising above all, blue peaks of mountains.

"Oh, Mother," he said, "untie the apron string and let me go!"

But the mother said, "Not yet, my child! Only yesterday you stumbled and would have fallen but for the apron string. Wait yet a little, until you are stronger."

So the boy waited, and all went as before. And the mother sang at her work.

But one day the boy found the door of the house standing open, for it was spring weather. He stood on the threshold and looked across the valley and saw the green trees waving, and the swift-flowing river with the sun flashing on it, and the blue mountains rising beyond. This time he heard the voice of the river calling, and it said, "Come!"

Then the boy started forward, and as he started, the string of the apron broke.

"Oh! How weak my mother's apron string is!" cried the boy and he ran out into the world, the broken string hanging beside him.

The mother gathered up the other end of the string and put it in her pocket and went about her work again. But she sang no more.

The boy ran on and on, rejoicing in his freedom and in the fresh air and the morning sun. He crossed the valley and began to climb the foothills. There the river flowed swiftly among rocks and cliffs. First it was easy climbing and then it was steep and craggy, but always he looked upward at the blue peaks beyond, and always the voice of the river was in his ears, saying, "Come!"

By and by he came to the brink of a precipice, over which the river dashed in a cataract, foaming and flashing and sending up clouds of silver spray. The spray filled his eyes so that he did not see his footing clearly. He grew dizzy, stumbled, and fell. But as he fell, something caught on a point of rock at the edge of the precipice, and held him, so that he hung dangling over the abyss. When he put up his hand to see what held him, he found that it was the broken string of the apron, which still hung by his side.

"Oh! How strong my mother's apron string is!" said the boy. He drew himself up by it and stood firm on his feet. Then he went on climbing toward the blue peaks of the mountains.

## NEVER-TELLS
## AND TATTLE-TALES

Some friends are little Tattle-Tales,
And some just never peep.
The Never-Tells make lovely friends,
All secrets they will keep.

Beware of chatty Tattle-Tales,
I'm warning you ahead;
They tattle everything you say,
And things you never said.

# THE SAILOR MAN

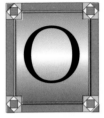

O nce upon a time two children came to the house of a sailor man, who lived beside the salt sea. They found the sailor man sitting in his doorway knotting his ropes.

"How do you do?" asked the sailor man.

"We are very well, thank you," said the children, who had learned manners, "and we hope you are the same. We heard that you have a boat, and we thought that perhaps you would take us out in her, and teach us how to sail. That is what we wish most to know."

"All in good time," said the sailor man. "I am busy now, but by and by, when my work is done, I may perhaps take one of you if you are ready to learn. Meantime here are some ropes that need knotting. You might be doing that, since it has to be done." And he showed them how the knots should be tied and went away and left them.

When he was gone the first child ran to the window and looked out.

"There is the sea," he said. "The waves come up on the beach, almost to the door of the house. They run up all white, like prancing horses, and then they go dragging back. Come and look!"

"I cannot," said the other child. "I am tying a knot."

"Oh!" cried the first child, "I see the boat. She is dancing like a lady at the ball. I never saw such a beauty. Come and Look!"

"I cannot," said the second child. "I am tying a knot."

"I shall have a delightful sail in that boat," said the first child. "I expect that the sailor man will take me, because I am the eldest and I know more about it. There was no need of my watching when he showed you the knots because I knew how already."

Just then the sailor man came in.

"Well," he said, "my work is done. What have you been doing in the meantime?"

"I have been looking at the boat," said the first child. "What a beauty she is! I shall have the best time in her that ever I have had in my life."

"I have been tying knots," said the second child.

"Come, then," said the sailor man, and he held out his hand to the second child. "I will take you out in the boat and teach you to sail her.

"But I am the eldest," cried the first child, "and I know a great deal more than she does."

"That may be," said the sailor man, "but a person must learn to tie a knot before he can learn to sail a boat."

"But I have learned to tie a knot," cried the child. "I know all about it!"

"How can I know that?" the sailor man asked.

## SHAMELESS ABEL

Once there was a boy named Abel
Who often spilled his food at table.
He had a dainty sister, Dot,
Who never made one single spot.
Their mother taught them both the same,
But Abel had no sense of shame.

# THE ROAD

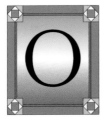nce upon a time a boy was going on a journey to the Great City. His family gathered at the door to bid him good-bye.

"Be sure you take the right road," said his mother.

"No fear," said his sister. "He is sure to do that."

"There is but one good road," said the old grandfather, who sat in the corner, "that is the straight road that runs up the hill."

The boy laughed, and kissed the grandfather on the forehead.

"You are a dear old grandfather," he said, "but you forget more than you remember. The road that I shall take is the one that goes through the flowering fields and beside the cool river."

He bade them all farewell and went forth with a light heart, for it was morning and the sun was shining clear. He made his way through the flowering fields, and it was beautiful there. The air was full of bird songs and the grass glittered with blossoms like a king's treasure chamber. They were red and blue and purple and the boy gathered one, then threw it away to gather another, and sang as he went.

After awhile he felt the ground wet and soft beneath his feet. The grass grew long, climbing about his knees and tangling his feet. At every step he sank deeper in mud and slime, and black bog water bubbled up around him. He realized that he was in a bottomless and treacherous morass. Moreover, when he looked around him the morass stretched far ahead and on every side, and there was no path through it.

"It is strange," said the boy, "that I did not see this morass before. I must go back or I shall lose my way, and perhaps my life."

With care and pain he dragged his feet out of the slough and made his way back to firm land. When he turned his face in the opposite direction, he saw the great hill rising before him, and over the hill a road ran straight among rocks and brambles.

"That looks like a hard road," said the boy, "but it must be a good one, for it is straight and dry. I will take that next time."

At nightfall the boy reached his home, weary and bedraggled.

"That was a wretched road I took this morning," he said. "Tomorrow I shall start again and take the straight road that runs over the hill, for that is the only good one."

"Is it, truly?" said the old grandfather, who sat in the corner. "That is good to know."

The boy laughed, and kissed him on his forehead.

"You are a dear old grandfather," he said, "but you forget more than you remember."

# THE LITTLE STAY-UP

Once there was a little girl,
Who would not go to bed,
Each night she got a scolding—
This willful sleepyhead.

She'd fall asleep right in her
chair,
Which was a great mistake,
Instead of feeling fine next day—
She could not keep awake.

# THE WILLING PRACTICER

When Ann sits down to practice
Her music every day,
She does it without urging,
And once I heard her say:
"I think I should be quite ashamed
If I should grow up tall—
And I were asked to play a piece
And I couldn't play at all!"

# CHILD'S PLAY

nce a child was sitting and playing on a great log that lay by the roadside. Another child soon came along and stopped to speak to him.

"What are you doing?" asked the second child.

"I am sailing to the Southern Seas," replied the first, "to get a cargo of monkeys, and elephant tusks, and crystal balls as large as oranges. Come up here, and you may sail with me if you like."

So the second child climbed upon the log.

"Look!" said the first child. "See how the foam bubbles up before the ship and trails and floats away behind! Look! The water is so clear that we can see the fishes swimming about, blue and red and green. There goes a parrot fish. My father told me about them. I would not be surprised if we saw a whale in about a minute."

"What are you talking about?" asked the second child, peevishly. "There is no water here, only grass. And anyhow this is nothing but a log. You cannot get to islands in this way."

"But we *have* got to them," cried the first child. "We are at them now. I see the palm trees waving and the white sand glittering. Look! There are the natives gathering to welcome us on the beach. They have feather cloaks and necklaces, and anklets of copper as red as gold. Oh! And there is an elephant coming straight toward us."

"I certainly think you would be ashamed of yourself," said the second child. "That is Widow Slocum."

"It's all the same," said the first child.

Presently the second child got down from the log.

"I am going to play with my toys," he said. "I don't see any sense in this. I think you are pretty dull to play things that aren't really there." And he walked slowly away.

The first child looked after him a moment. "I think *you* are pretty dull," he said to himself, "to see nothing but what is under your nose." But he was too well-mannered to say this aloud; and having taken aboard his cargo he sailed for another port.

# Susan Kindly's Party

Susan planned a birthday party;
The invitations read:
"No presents please, dear  friends
        of mine!"
She planned to *give* instead.

So when Susan's birthday came
All her friends were there,
And Susan gave each one a toy—
It was a grand affair.

# A MISUNDERSTANDING

nce a child who thought well of herself was walking along the street and saw another child, who was poorly clad. "How wretched it must be," she said to herself, "to be poor and shabby like that child! How thin she is! And how her patched cloak flutters in the wind; so different from my velvet dress and coat."

Just then an Angel came along.

"What are you looking at?" asked the Angel.

"I was looking at that girl!" said the child.

"So was I," said the Angel. "How beautifully she is dressed!"

"What do you mean?" asked the child.

"She is dressed in rags, or at least if her clothes are not ragged, they are wretchedly thin and shabby."

"Oh, no," said the Angel. "How can you say so? She is in sparkling white, as clear as frost. I never saw anything so pretty. But you, you poor little thing, you are indeed miserably clad. Does not the wind blow through and through these flimsy tatters? But at least you could keep them clean, my dear, and mended. You should see to that."

"I don't know what you can mean!" said the child. "That girl is a ragged beggar and my father is the richest man in town. I'm wearing a velvet dress and lovely coat trimmed with expensive fur. What are you talking about?"

"I am talking about the clothes of your soul, of course!" said the Angel, who was very young.

"I don't know anything about souls," said the child.

"I certainly didn't think you did!" said the Angel.

# THE ORDERLY TWINS

When Ray and May come in from school,
Or when they come from play—
They clean their shoes well on the mat
And put their coats away.

Of course they play and romp a lot,
And have just stacks of fun;
But they put all their games away
When playing time is done.

# THE STARS

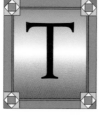 little dear child lay in his crib and sobbed, because he was afraid of the dark. And his father, in the room below, heard the sobs, and came up, and said, "What ails you, my dearie, and why do you cry?"

And the child said, "Oh, Father, I am afraid of the dark. Nurse says I am too big to have a candle, but all the corners are full of dreadful blackness, and I think there are Things in them with eyes that would look at me if I looked at them. And if they looked at me I should die. Oh, Father, why is it dark? Why is there such a terrible thing as darkness? Why cannot it be always day?

The father took the child in his arms and carried him downstairs and out into the summer night.

"Look up, dearie!" he said, in his strong, kind voice. "Look up, and see God's little lights!"

The little one looked up and saw the stars, spangling the blue veil of the sky. Bright as candles they burned, and yellow as gold.

"Oh, Father," cried the child, "what are those lovely things?"

"Those are stars," said the father. "Those are God's little lights."

"But why have I never seen them before?"

"Because you are a very little child and have never been out in the night before."

"Can I see the stars only at night, Father?"

"Only at night, my child!"

"Do they only come then, Father?"

"No, they are always there, but we cannot see them when the sun is shining."

"But Father, the darkness is not terrible here, it is beautiful!"

"Yes, dearie. The darkness is always beautiful, if we will only look up at the stars, instead of into the corners."

# THE SLEEP ANGEL

Hist! Hist! My little lambikin,
The time for play is gone—
Sleep fairies beckon us to bed
Come, get your nightie on.

All kindly children have sweet dreams
The Sleep Angel from her throne
Smiles down on every kindly heart.
She calls each one her own.